For **Peyton** and *Seth*

The Repairman

Written and Illustrated by

Joel Wilson

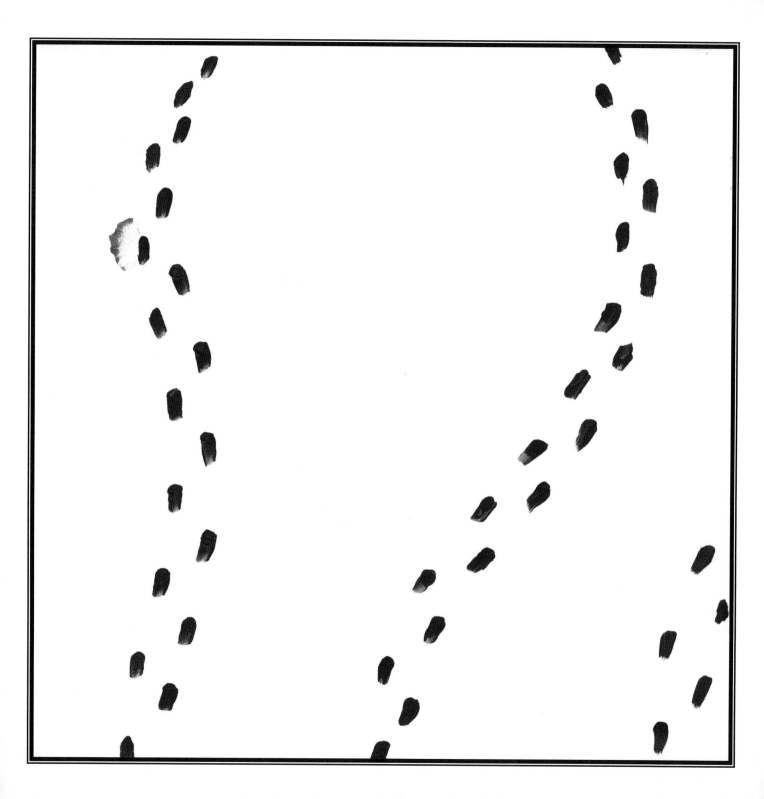

Welcome to the land of Monotony.

These little people are the Monotones.

They always do exactly what they are told,

and they are always told exactly what to do.

They all look similar; don't they?

They act the same too.

This guy is a sign repairman.

Like every other good Monotone,

he follows the same path every day. But, just in case he forgets where he is going, there is always a reminder nearby. Those signs are everywhere! They must always be very easy to read.

So, his job is really important.

He has to work hard every day because there are so many signs that need upkeep.

It seems like every morning, when he gets to the factory, the stack of signs gets bigger, and his bottle of ink gets smaller.

When it's finally time to go home, he's beat.

But he knows that he is not supposed to complain, so he just lowers his head and watches his feet fall into the same old path.

Soon, he'll be home. With a good night's sleep, he will wake up refreshed and ready to work, right?

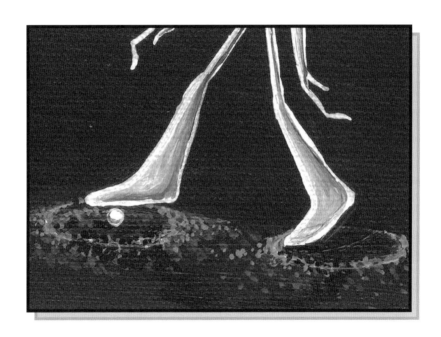

Not this time.

Today, a tiny round stone has fallen right into his path. His next step zips awkwardly over the stone, sending our little Monotone friend flailing out of control...

...and he lands, face first,

on the cold, hard ground.

It really shakes up his head. As he slowly picks himself off the ground, he tries to gather his sense of direction.

It's useless; he can't even see the demanding signs that scream at him to get back in line.

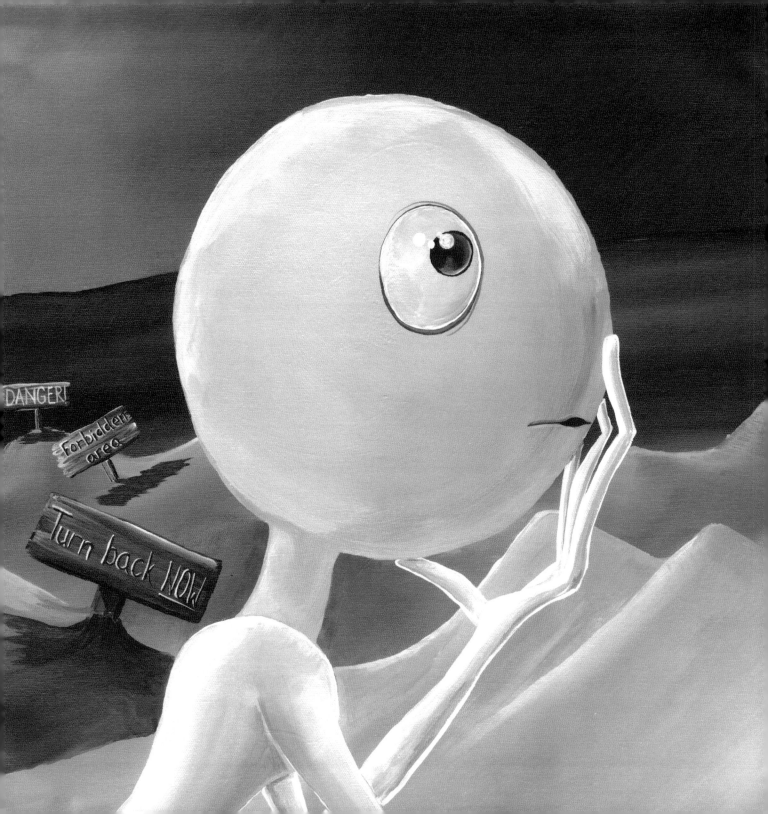

When he finally opens his eyes, he sees something amazing.

Even though everything he has ever known is telling him to turn around and walk away, he can't, he won't.

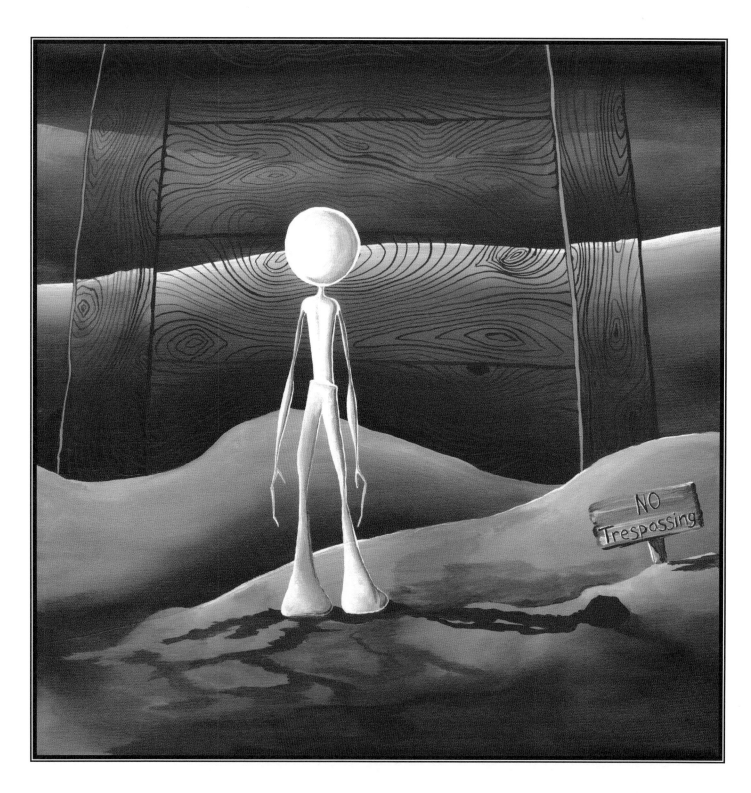

"What is this, a barrier?"

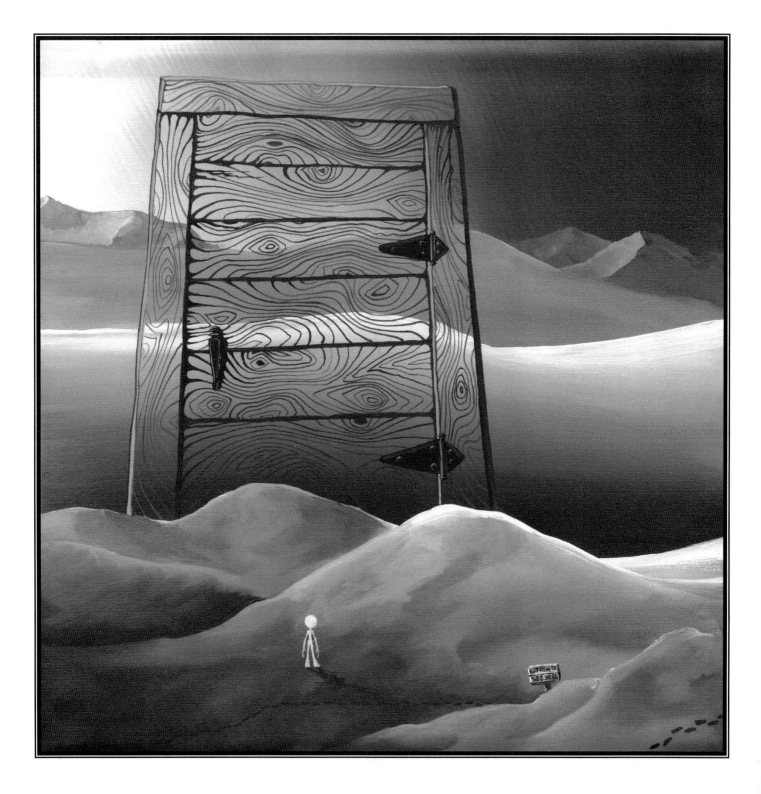

"No, it's a doorway. So... what's on the other side?"

Things are about to change.

He stares at the doorway for a long time as thoughts flood into his mind.

Then, with a smile on his face, he walks home, excited to know that there is more to this world than he ever imagined.

He doesn't even pay attention

to the signs that bark

the same old, tired orders at him,

as they had always done.

He is too busy thinking

of what might be

beyond that doorway.

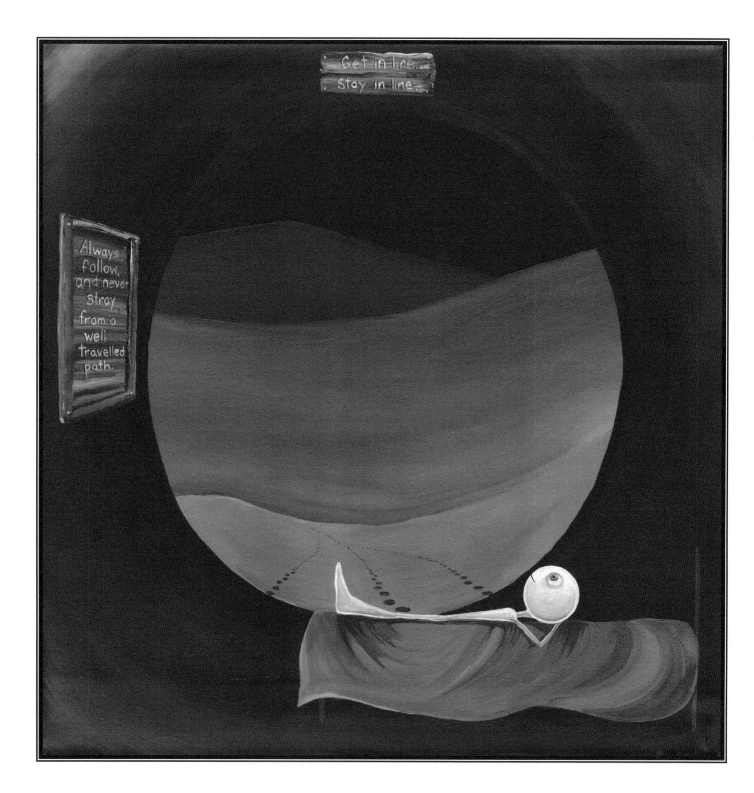

When he gets home and lies down for the night,

his mind is still racing.

Those signs are persistent,
and they remind him that the well-traveled path
has always been good enough.
They make a strong argument...

...but not strong enough.

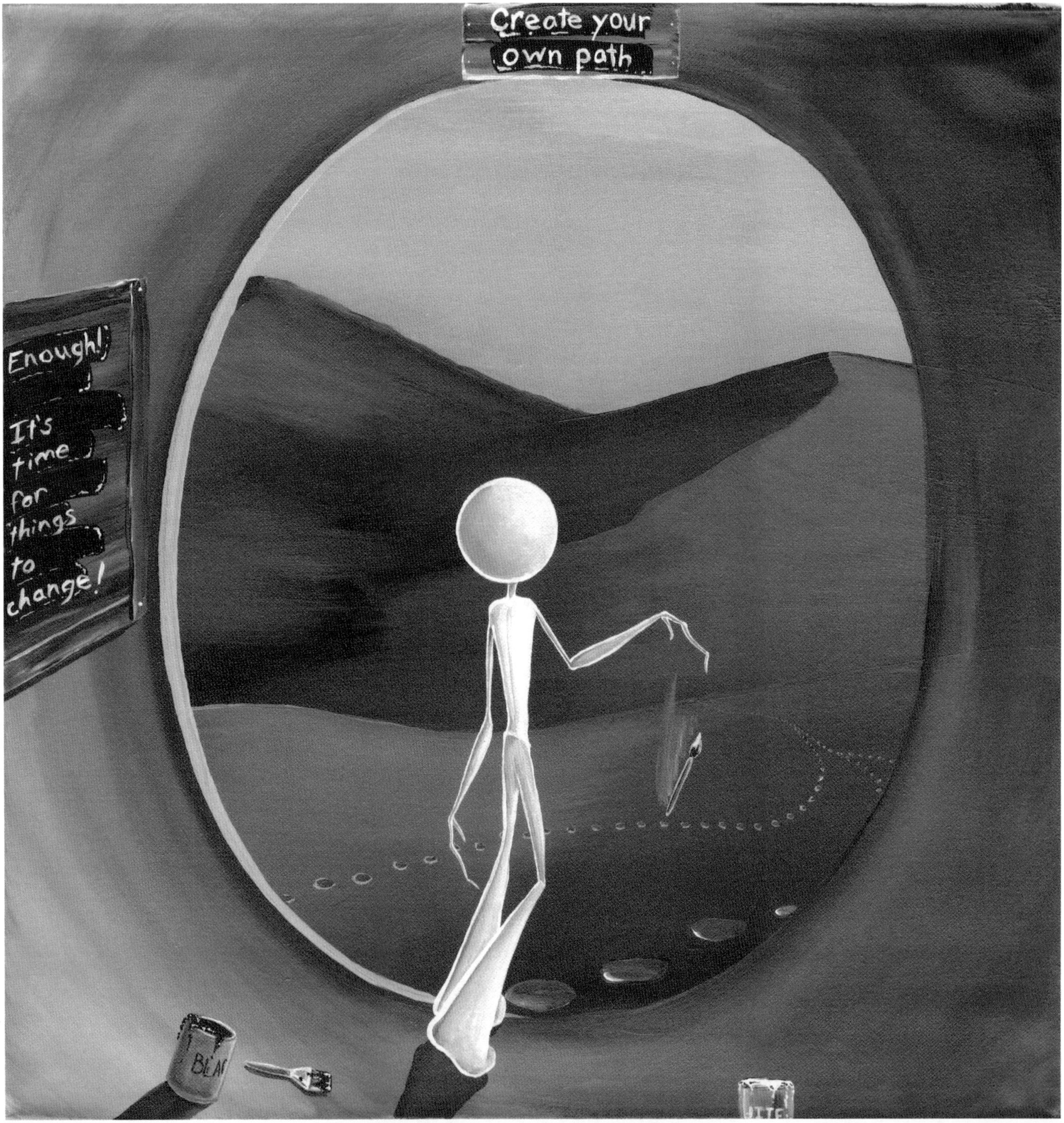
Create your own path
Enough!
It's time for things to change!

He has something

to say too,

so he repairs some signs.

His words are powerful...

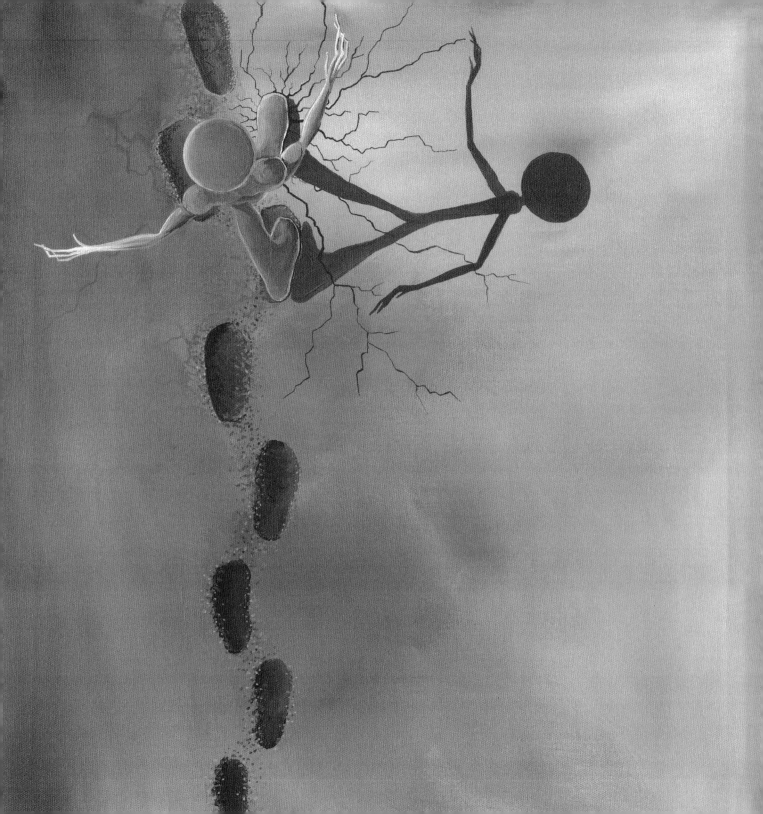

. . .and so are his actions.

With a heart full of courage,

he takes the first step

of a brand new path.

It seems that he is not the only one ready for change. Others follow his lead, ignoring the signs that tell them to stay in line.

They are amazed and confused

by what he shows them.

But, more importantly, they are curious. They decide to open this door to see what is on the other side.

But they are just little Monotones and this is one massive door.

They can't budge it.

They can't even dig under, or go around it.

The signs mock their efforts.

Perhaps they should listen, and get back to the normal routine.

The door seems to look down on him,

but the repairman knows he is more than

just a little Monotone.

He won't back down.

He grins, clinches his fist,

and swings with determination.

"Crack!"

echoes throughout the land.

The signs seem desperate now,

and soon, the reason is clear.

The barrier begins to fall apart. So does the land of Monotony.

The little people that once

referred to themselves as Monotones

are suddenly

full of hope and wonder.

The signs begin to change.

The old paths fade away.

Everybody would soon be making their own.

BE BRAVE

TAKE A STAND

BE YOURSELF

And be the one
lead the way

It's good to be a repairman...

when there are

things that need to be fixed.